# Franklin and the Thunderstorm

For my neighbor, Amanda — P. B.

For my mother, who still worries
about thunderstorms — B. C.

Franklin is a trademark of Kids Can Press Ltd.

Text © 1998 Contextx Inc.
Illustrations © 1998 Brenda Clark Illustrator Inc.
Interior illustrations prepared with the assistance of Shelley Southern
and Muriel Hughes Wood.

Kids Can Press acknowledges the financial support of the Ontario
Arts Council; the Canada Council for the Arts and the Government
of Canada, through the CBF, for our publishing activity.

Published in Canada by        Published in the U.S. by
Kids Can Press Ltd.           Kids Can Press Ltd.
25 Dockside Drive             2250 Military Road
Toronto, ON  M5A 0B5          Tonawanda, NY 14150

www.kidscanpress.com

The hardcover edition of this book is smyth sewn casebound.
The paperback edition of this book is limp sewn with a drawn-on cover.
Manufactured in Buji, Shenzhen, China, in 3/2016 by WKT Company

CM 98  0 9 8 7 6 5 4 3 2
CDN PA 98  0 9
CMC PA 16  0 9 8 7 6 5 4 3 2 1

**Library and Archives Canada Cataloguing in Publication**

Bourgeois, Paulette
   Franklin and the thunderstorm / written by Paulette Bourgeois ;
illustrated by Brenda Clark.

(A classic Franklin story)
ISBN 978-1-55453-729-7

1. Franklin (Fictitious character : Bourgeois) — Juvenile fiction.
I. Clark, Brenda  II. Title.

PS8553.O85477F54 2011        jC813'.54        C2010-906675-8

Kids Can Press is a *lorus*™ Entertainment company

# Franklin and the Thunderstorm

*Written by* Paulette Bourgeois
*Illustrated by* Brenda Clark

Kids Can Press

FRANKLIN could count by twos and tie his shoes. He could name the months of the year and all the seasons. He could read the thermometer, and he checked the barometer every day. Franklin worried about the weather because he was afraid of storms.

One day, Franklin was supposed to play at Fox's house, but the sky was getting dark and the clouds were thick.

"Maybe I shouldn't go," Franklin said to his mother.

She looked out the window. "It probably won't rain until later," she said. "You have time to get to Fox's."

Franklin put on his boots and took the umbrella.

As Franklin hurried to Fox's house, he kept looking at the sky. The clouds moved quickly, and wind swirled dirt in the air.

Franklin felt all jumpy inside.

Fox was playing outside when Franklin arrived.

Franklin pointed nervously to the sky. "I think we should go inside, don't you?" he asked.

"Not yet." Fox grinned. "I love watching the clouds move and feeling the wind blow. It's exciting!"

"I think it's scary," said Franklin.

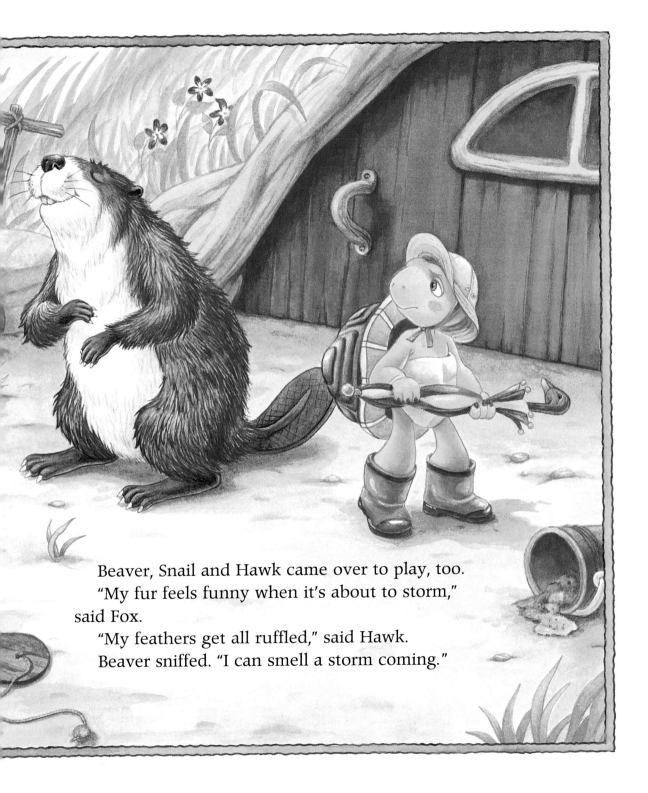

Beaver, Snail and Hawk came over to play, too.

"My fur feels funny when it's about to storm," said Fox.

"My feathers get all ruffled," said Hawk.

Beaver sniffed. "I can smell a storm coming."

The wind became stronger.
Hawk flew loop-the-loops. "Whee!" he cried.
Franklin held on to his hat and shivered.
It was almost as dark as night when big fat
raindrops began to fall.
"We should go in!" shouted Franklin.
"No," said Fox. "Follow me."

They raced to the tree house, where it was dry.

"Fox!" called his mother. "Time for everyone to come in."

"It's all right," Fox shouted back. "We're in the tree."

Fox's mother was there in a second. "It's dangerous to be near a tree during a storm," she said. "Lightning strikes tall things first, and you might get hurt."

Franklin held on to Fox's mother all the way from the tree to the house. They were barely in the door when there was a flash of zigzag light.

"Lightning!" shrieked Franklin. He trembled.

KA-BOOM!

"Thunder!" he screamed.

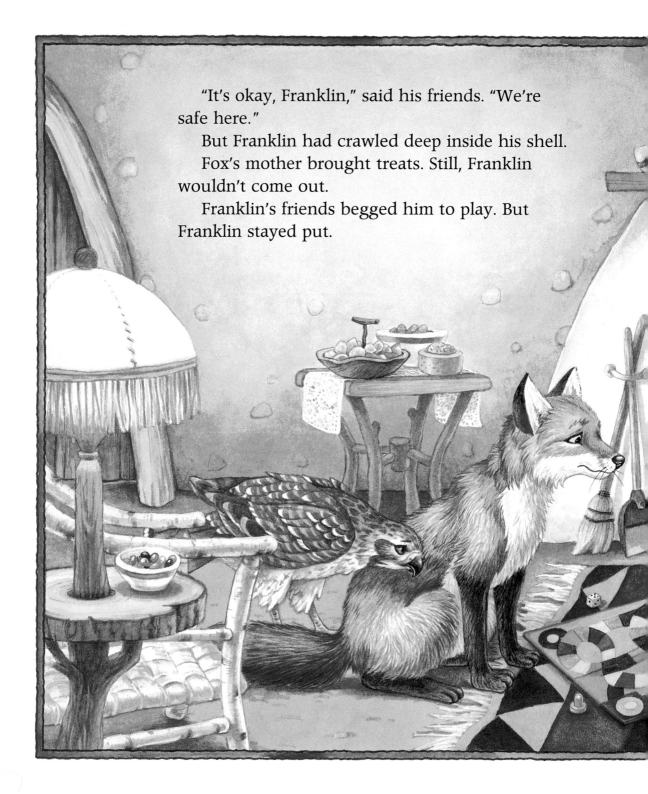

"It's okay, Franklin," said his friends. "We're safe here."

But Franklin had crawled deep inside his shell.

Fox's mother brought treats. Still, Franklin wouldn't come out.

Franklin's friends begged him to play. But Franklin stayed put.

Then, with a flash and a crash, the lights went out.

"Don't worry," said Fox's mother. She lit candles and turned on a flashlight.

"Won't you come out now?" she asked Franklin.

"No, thank you," he mumbled.

"Don't be afraid," said Hawk. "All that noise is just cloud giants playing drums in the sky."

Franklin peeked out. "Really?" he asked.

"No, it's not," giggled Snail. "That noise is made when the giants go bowling."

Franklin came out of his shell. "But what about the lightning?"

"That's easy," said Hawk. "The cloud giants are turning their lights on and off."

Fox smiled. "I think it's the giants swinging from their chandeliers."

Franklin laughed.

"Giants! That's ridiculous," said Beaver. "Mr. Owl says lightning is a big spark of electricity that travels from the sky to the ground. The spark is so hot that it makes the air around it POP! That's the sound of thunder."

"Amazing!" said Franklin.

Franklin felt a little better. He even played flashlight tag with his friends.

Soon, there was hardly any lightning. The thunder was a low rumble from far away, and the rain stopped.

Then the lights went on.

"Storm's over!" said Fox. "Let's go outside and play."

"Look," said Franklin. "A rainbow!"

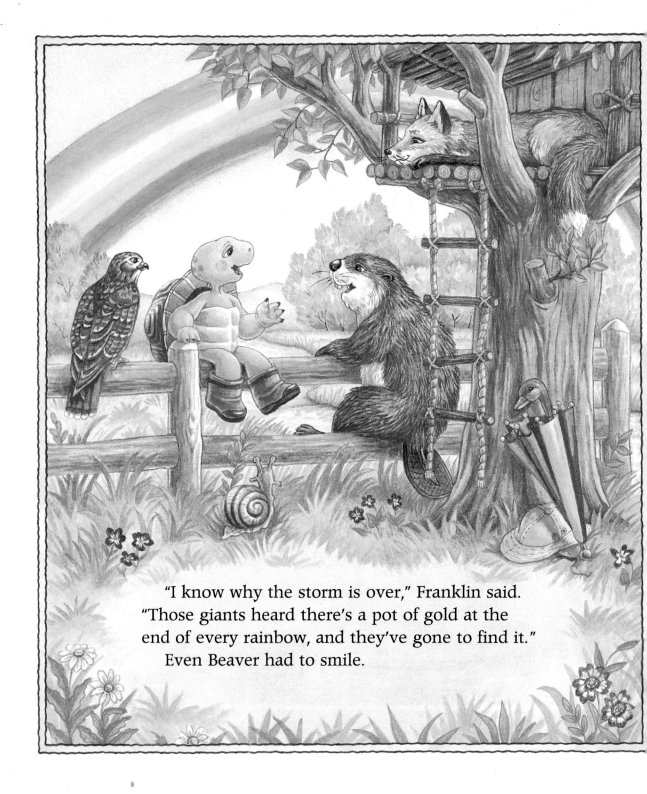

"I know why the storm is over," Franklin said.
"Those giants heard there's a pot of gold at the
end of every rainbow, and they've gone to find it."
Even Beaver had to smile.